BULGY

Based on *The Railway Ser* Iry

Illustrations by
Robin Davies and Jerry Smith

EGMONT

EGMONT

We bring stories to life

First published in Great Britain in 2003
by Egmont UK Limited
239 Kensington High Street, London W8 6SA
This edition published in 2008
All Rights Reserved

Thomas the Tank Engine & Friends™

CREATED BY BRITT ALLCROFT

HiT entertainment

ISBN 978 1 4052 3451 1
1 3 5 7 9 10 8 6 4 2
Printed in Italy

The Forest Stewardship Council (FSC) is an international, non-governmental organisation dedicated to promoting responsible management of the world's forests. FSC operates a system of forest certification and product labelling that allows consumers to identify wood and wood-based products from well managed forests.

For more information about Egmont's paper buying policy please visit www.egmont.co.uk/ethicalpublishing

For more information about the FSC please visit their website at www.fsc.uk.org

This is a story about Bulgy the bus. He came to work on the Island of Sodor during the busy season. He thought he was better than all the engines, so he tried to take their passengers away ...

It was the sightseeing season on the Island of Sodor. The Fat Controller's engines were working hard. Their station was crowded with people.

Duck, Donald and Douglas were taking passengers from the station to other parts of the Island. Some passengers had been brought to Sodor by a big, red bus called Bulgy.

Bulgy looked at the crowded platform and frowned.

"I wouldn't have brought more passengers if I'd known how many were here already," he said.

"But they are all really enjoying themselves," said Duck.

"Pah!" replied Bulgy, crossly.

Duck thought Bulgy was very moody.

Bulgy was rude to all the engines. Every time he saw them, he shouted, "Down with the railways!" He said railways should be closed so coaches, buses and cars could do everything instead!

The engines thought Bulgy was rather silly. But when another bus arrived to take Bulgy's passengers home, the engines were worried. This meant Bulgy was going to stay on the Island. Would he really get the railway closed down? What would the engines do then?

Bulgy told the passengers that he could get them to the Big Station faster than the engines could.

"That's rubbish!" said Duck. "It's much further by road."

"Yes," said Oliver, "but Bulgy says he knows a short cut."

That evening, Duck was about to start his final journey of the day, but he only had a few passengers aboard. He waited for a few minutes, hoping more would turn up, but none did.

Just then, Duck heard a loud, "Toot! Toot!" Bulgy was leaving the station. He had a sign on his side saying 'RAILWAY BUS'. Most of Duck's passengers had gone with Bulgy because he had told them he was working for the railway.

"Stop!" called the railway staff, as Bulgy pulled away, but it was too late.

"Yah! Boo! Snubs!" Bulgy said, as he roared away with the passengers.

Duck and his carriages, Alice and Mirabel, set off on their journey with the few passengers they had.

"Bulgy is a nasty old thief!" said Alice to Mirabel. "He's taken our people."

Duck knew they had to stop Bulgy taking their passengers. If it carried on like this, the railway could be shut down! He wondered what they should do.

But Bulgy was about to be stopped. His short cut led down a narrow road with a low bridge. As he rushed under the bridge, there was a sudden screeching noise and he ground to a halt. He tried to move forwards and he tried to move backwards but it was no good. He was totally stuck! Cars and coaches beeped angrily at Bulgy because he was blocking the road.

"A tall bus like you should never have gone down this road!" they said.

Bulgy's passengers were furious.

"We should have gone with Duck!" they said. "He would never have let us down like this. We're going to miss our train at the Big Station and it's all your fault," they shouted at Bulgy.

Bulgy didn't say a word.

As Duck reached the bridge, a man appeared by the track, waving a red warning flag.

"Danger!" he cried. "A bus is stuck under the bridge."

Duck moved slowly forward. He saw Bulgy under the bridge.

"So, that is Bulgy's so-called short cut!" he laughed.

Bulgy held his breath as Duck slowly moved over the bridge.

"The bus tricked us!" said Bulgy's passengers. "He said he was working for the railway, but he lied! Can we go with you instead?"

Duck agreed and took all the passengers to the Big Station in time for their train. The passengers promised they would always travel by train from then on.

Bulgy was left under the bridge. He had to wait all night before he was rescued. He didn't learn his lesson though; he still thought he could take over the railway.

But by then, everyone knew that it was faster to go by train so they all travelled with the engines instead.

DANGER
LOW BRIDGE

FREE
THE
ROADS

Bulgy decided to retire. He asked a farmer if he could live in his field and look after his hens. The farmer agreed.

From that day on, Bulgy was much happier. The hens enjoyed hearing about his grand adventures on the bus route, and how terrible engines were. They didn't know any better! And Bulgy felt proud because the hens produced more eggs than ever before.

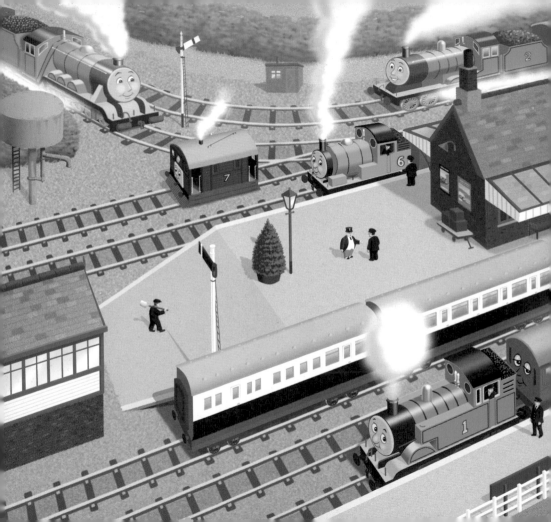

The Thomas Story Library is THE definitive collection of stories about Thomas and ALL his friends.

5 more Thomas Story Library titles will be chuffing into your local bookshop in August 2008!

Jeremy
Hector
BoCo
Billy
Whiff

And there are even more Thomas Story Library books to follow later

So go on, start your Thomas Story Library NOW!

A Fantastic Offer for Thomas the Tank Engine Fans!

In every Thomas Story Library book like this one, you will find a special token. Collect 6 Thomas tokens and we will send you a brilliant Thomas poster, and a double-sided bedroom door hanger! Simply tape a £1 coin in the space above, and fill out the form overleaf.

Cut along the dotted line

TO BE COMPLETED BY AN ADULT

To apply for this great offer, ask an adult to complete the coupon below and send it with a pound coin and 6 tokens, to:
THOMAS OFFERS, PO BOX 715, HORSHAM RH12 5WG

☐ Please send a Thomas poster and door hanger. I enclose 6 tokens plus a £1 coin. (Price includes P&P)

Fan's name...

Address..

....Postcode.............................

Date of birth..

Name of parent/guardian...

Signature of parent/guardian..

Please allow 28 days for delivery. Offer is only available while stocks last. We reserve the right to change the terms of this offer at any time and we offer a 14 day money back guarantee. This does not affect your statutory rights.

☐ Data Protection Act: If you do not wish to receive other similar offers from us or companies we recommend, please tick this box. Offers apply to UK only.

Cut along the dotted line